Winning Ways in
SOCCER

Janet Grosshandler

PHOTOGRAPHS BY THE AUTHOR

COBBLEHILL BOOKS
Dutton • New York

For Nate, Jeff, and Mike
—and especially Hank

Copyright © 1991 by Janet Grosshandler
All rights reserved
No part of this book may be reproduced in any form
without permission in writing from the publisher.

Library of Congress Cataloging-in-Publication Data
Grosshandler, Janet.
Winning ways in soccer / Janet Grosshandler ; photographs
by the author.
p.   cm.
Summary: Text and photographs demonstrate how soccer is
played and how players learn skills and sportsmanship.
ISBN 0-525-65064-4
1. Soccer—Juvenile literature. [1. Soccer.] I. Title.
GV943.25.G74   1991   796.334′2—dc20
90-48620   CIP   AC

Published in the United States by Cobblehill Books,
an affiliate of Dutton Children's Books,
a division of Penguin Books USA Inc.
Designed by Jean Krulis
Printed in Hong Kong
First Edition   10 9 8 7 6 5 4 3 2 1

Girls and boys ages five to eight, who want to
learn how to play soccer, can join a soccer team.

You don't have to know how to play soccer
already. The coach will help you learn the game.
In soccer you have to get the ball down the field
and try to score a goal without using your hands!

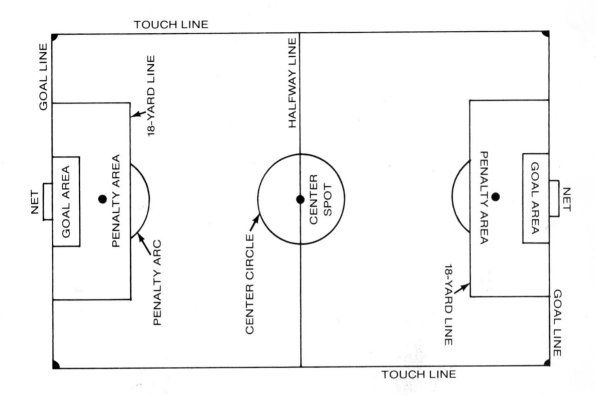

Here is the field we play on. It is a big field. You have to run a lot in soccer.

Only eleven players on a team can play during a game. We have special positions. To win, your team has to get the ball into the other team's net—and not let them get it into yours.

We have to wear special equipment to play.

Our shoes have cleats that help us dig in and run faster. Shin guards protect our legs if we get kicked by another player.

Best of all, we get team shirts! We call our team the Rockets. "Go, Rockets!"

Our coach teaches us soccer skills at team practice. Kicking the ball with your feet is hard. Sometimes we miss. But when we get a good foot on it—POW! The ball can go way down the field.

The hardest thing to remember is not to use our hands. We forget sometimes.

Dribbling the ball is when we move it down the field by using very short kicks. You try to keep the ball close to your feet and control it. That's not as easy as it looks.

If we want to pass the ball to a teammate, we kick it hard. In soccer you kick with the top of your foot where the shoelaces are. Good players can kick with either foot.

If we want to stop the ball from getting past us, we have to trap it.

We learn to trap with our feet, our chest, and the thigh part (top) of our leg.

It's scary to jump out and try to stop a fast-moving ball. But after we do it once, we get better.

We can't use our hands in soccer, but we can use our heads. Heading the ball is when we use our forehead to send the ball down the field or into the goal.

It's hard to keep your eye on the ball and head it at the same time.

We don't do this much, but it is fun to try.

Our coach teaches us to play the different positions in a soccer game. We change around so we can learn to play all the positions.

It's hard to wait our turn on the sideline, but sometimes it's nice to have a rest and cheer our team on.

The goalkeeper, or goalie, has to stop the ball from going into the net. The goalie is the only player who can use his or her hands. The goalie can kick (punt) the ball or throw it back onto the field to start the game up again after the ball is caught.

When you catch the ball to stop a goal, you feel great! When the other team gets the ball into the net—that's not much fun.

The forwards are attacking players. They are the front line of the team, and play near the net. They try to score goals.

Everyone likes to score, but it is tougher than it looks. The other team does its best to keep your shot out of the goal. You have to shoot quickly and try to get the ball past their goalie and into the net.

The halfbacks play the middle of the field. They do a lot of running and try to pass the ball up to the forwards.

Halfbacks can shoot for goals if they are close enough and have the chance. There's always lots of action for the halfbacks. We have to use all our skills—dribbling, passing, trapping, heading—to get that soccer ball down the field toward the goal.

The fullbacks defend the goal. They are the last ones on the team to clear the ball away from our goal to keep the other team from scoring.

Our fullbacks give big kicks to send the soccer ball back to our halfbacks and away from our goal.

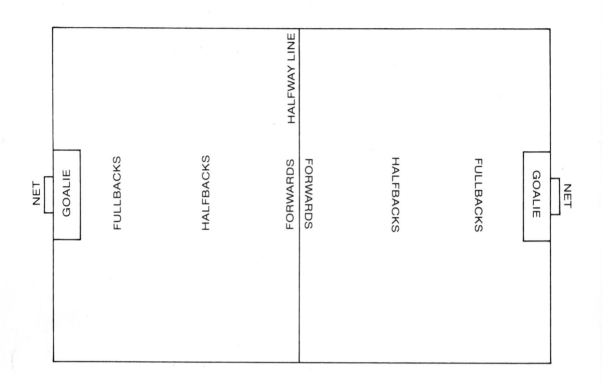

This is how we line up on the field. Our coach always has to remind us to stay in our positions. That means we play our own part of the field and don't run all over the place. Sometimes we get so excited we forget.

At one practice game our goalie ran down to the other team's net and tried to score!

When the other team kicks the ball out of bounds, we do a throw-in. A throw-in has to be done a special way, or the referee will give the ball back to the other team.

We hold the ball over our head. Both feet must be on the ground.

Ready? Throw it straight onto the field! Always throw the ball toward your own goal, even if you are far away from it.

The referee makes sure that our game is played fairly and safely. He or she will call us for fouls if we break the soccer game rules. The referee will take the ball away and give it to the other team.

These are fouls:

Pushing—Do not use your arms or body to push another player.

Tripping—You cannot trip a player from the other team.

Dangerous play—Do not do something that could hurt another player, such as kicking the ball when someone is on the ground nearby.

High kick—When you kick, be careful that you do not kick so high that your foot is near a player's head, face, or upper body.

Hand ball—Never touch the ball with your hands while you are on the field.

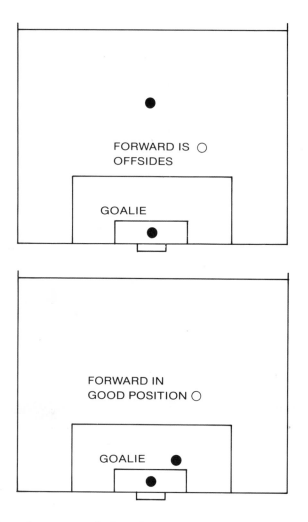

FORWARD IS ○
OFFSIDES

GOALIE

FORWARD IN
GOOD POSITION ○

GOALIE

Offsides is one of the hardest rules to remember. If we want to pass the ball to a teammate, and we are in the other team's end of the field, we have to have two players from the other team between us and the goal. (One can be the goalie.) If we don't, then we are offsides.

When a rule is broken, the ref gives the other team a free kick.

A direct free kick means that we can shoot right at the goal from where the ref places the ball on the field. The other players must all stand back.

An indirect free kick means that the ball has to touch another player on our team before it can be shot into the goal.

The penalty area is inside the 18-yard line. If a foul is made inside the penalty area, the other team gets a penalty kick.

On a penalty kick, both teams have to stand back while one player kicks the ball right at the goal. The goalie is the only one there to try to stop it.

Being the goalie for a penalty kick is scary. It is tough to block that ball!

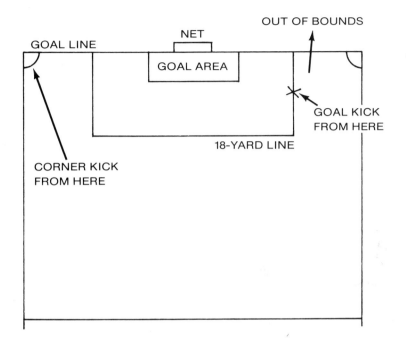

When the ball goes out of bounds behind the goal, there are two ways to bring it back in.

If *we* kicked it out behind our own goal, the other team kicks it back in from the corner. That's a corner kick.

If *they* kicked it out of bounds behind our goal, then we get to kick it upfield from the line on one side of our goal area. That's a goal kick.

We are ready to play a game! Our team captains go out onto the field for the coin toss. Whoever wins the toss gets to pick which goal they want to defend, and if they want to kick off.

In our games, we play two halves. At the end of a half, we change the goal we are defending.

Coach tells us to remember all we have learned and to play safely. We are ready! We line up on the field in our positions.

Go, Rockets! Kickoff!

We use all our soccer skills. We try passing, dribbling, kicking, trapping, shooting at the goal.

The first half goes by fast. We play hard to defend our goal.

Here comes our chance to shoot!
Score!
Yahoo! Rockets score a goal!

We are tired at halftime. Coach gives us some oranges for energy. Drinking a little water helps, too, especially on a hot day.

Coach says, "You Rockets are doing great! I see team play and good passing. Keep it up!

The whistle blows. Time for the second half.

Being the goalie during the second half is a tough
job. The other team wants to score.

We try to keep the ball out of our net, but they get
off a good shot. Score for them.

Now we are 1-1.

The referee blows the whistle to end the game. Time is over and we did not score again. It is a 1-1 tie.

That's okay because it was a good, close game. We used all our soccer skills to play the best we could.

We go out on the field and shake hands with the other team and say, "Good game! Good game!"

Coach is happy because we did our best. Did we have fun? Yes!

"Who are we?" Coach cheers.

"Rockets!" we yell.

"What do we play?"

"Soccer!"

"How do we play it?"

"Gr-r-r-r-reat!"

Time to go home. We are tired and happy. We can't wait until next week's game.

Go, Rockets!